James Hurley Pring

A Memoir of Thomas Chard

Suffragan Bishop and the Last Abbot of Ford Abbey, Dorsetshire ...

James Hurley Pring

A Memoir of Thomas Chard
Suffragan Bishop and the Last Abbot of Ford Abbey, Dorsetshire ...

ISBN/EAN: 9783337107338

Printed in Europe, USA, Canada, Australia, Japan

Cover: Foto ©Raphael Reischuk / pixelio.de

More available books at **www.hansebooks.com**

A

MEMOIR

OF

THOMAS CHARD, D.D.

SUFFRAGAN BISHOP,

AND THE

Last Abbot of Ford Abbey, Dorsetshire;

LATE IN THE COUNTY OF DEVON.

BY

JAMES HURLY PRING, M.D.

LONDON:

T. RICHARDS, 37, GREAT QUEEN STREET.
TAUNTON: F. MAY, HIGH STREET.

1864.

PREFACE.

THE following memoir was communicated to the Congress of the British Archæological Association at their meeting at Exeter in August 1861, when, with the omission of certain portions, it was read to the meeting, and was subsequently printed, with the same omissions, in the *Journal* of the Association for the following year; the chief part of what was thus omitted being that which related to Ford Abbey. A paper exclusively devoted to a description of the Abbey having been furnished to the meeting at the same time by one much better qualified than myself for the undertaking, it was deemed advisable, with the view, moreover, of avoiding anything like repetition, to omit from the Memoir of the Last Abbot those parts which were in any way descriptive of the Abbey; an arrangement which, however judicious in itself, and considerate towards the members of the Association, had the effect, as it appeared to me, of depriving my paper of some of its chief features of interest.

By the course adopted all description of the object with which his memory is most intimately associated, was excluded from the Memoir of the Last Abbot of Ford; whilst, as a necessary consequence, the Illustrations which were intended to accompany the description of some of those portions of the abbey which were the work of Dr. Chard, were rendered unavailable, and I was further precluded from making reference to certain architectural details on which I relied to establish some points relating to the Subject of the Memoir which had hitherto been held doubtful.

From a consideration of these circumstances, and a desire still to fulfil my first intention, I have been induced to reproduce the Memoir in its present form, with the omitted portions, and with the accompanying illustrations.

In addition to those in the original paper, a few notes have since been inserted; and it may here be observed, in reference to the account of Ford Abbey, that all that is designed is to furnish such a cursory general description of the abbey as may enable the reader the more readily to distinguish, and become acquainted with, the portions which are the work of the Last Abbot.

I would beg to refer those who may desire to obtain a more detailed account of the abbey, to a *History of Ford Abbey*, published anonymously in 1846, and to the paper on Ford Abbey by Mr. Gordon Hills, already referred to, which may be expected to appear in a forthcoming volume of the *Collectanea Archæologica*, but with which unfortunately I have not as yet had an opportunity of becoming acquainted. The illustrations have been very carefully executed by Mr. Clarke, having been drawn from actual inspection of the objects; aided, as regards the views of Ford Abbey, by the additional advantages afforded by photographic art.

J. H. P.

Taunton, 29th December, 1863.

A MEMOIR OF THOMAS CHARD, D.D.

SUFFRAGAN BISHOP, AND LAST ABBOT OF FORD ABBEY.

HE age in which we live is sufficiently remote from that great, absorbing event in the religious history of our country, the Reformation, to enable us to look back on the period of its enactment undisturbed by those fierce passions which it called into existence, and which it has required all the influence of the softening hand of time, even from that period to the present, to assuage. Viewed, however, from the vista in which the lapse of upwards of three centuries has served to enshroud the monastic institutions of our land, and aided by the presence of the genial though distant beams of enlightening charity, it is surprising, amidst the enormities charged upon them at the time by their spoilers, how much there now appears to have been connected with these establishments that commends itself to our reverence, and has a lasting claim upon our gratitude. To say that they were human institutions, and, as such, that even the influence of religion did not avail to exempt them, especially in a rude and semibarbarous age, from the abuses and corruption inseparable from all schemes of human device, is what must readily be conceded; though it is now becoming generally admitted that the instances of profligacy were the exception rather than the rule amongst them, and that these were eagerly seized upon and used for private ends by those interested in bringing the whole body into disrepute. With this admission, therefore, the spirit of religion will, it is

apprehended, be best fulfilled by dropping the veil of oblivion over those failings which these conventual establishments disclosed as incident to our common nature; and by
endeavouring rather to extract and dwell upon the good
they were undoubtedly the means not only of diffusing at
the time throughout the length and breadth of our land, but
also of transmitting as a sacred bequest to posterity.[1]

With this object it is that I am induced to endeavour to
delineate more fully than has yet been done the outlines,
now well nigh obliterated, of the life of an ecclesiastic of
those times, in the belief that it will be found to furnish
another instance, in addition to those already well known,
which may tend to relieve the body of the clergy of those
days from the unjust opprobrium which for a long period
it has been the custom too generally and indiscriminately
to heap upon them; whilst it will, at the same time, bring
us acquainted with many topics of great antiquarian interest
in the county of Devon.

In reviewing, then, the list of abbots of the once noted
monastery of Ford in Devonshire,[2] many of whom were eminent both for their piety and learning, the last—though it
may be truly said not the least illustrious amongst them—
was Thomas Chard, D.D., the subject of the present brief
memoir. His career, less conspicuous in the eye of the
world than that of his early predecessor, the famous Baldwin (who, from a humble origin,[3] rose through successive

<hr/>

[1] The justice of this latter remark has since received forcible illustration
from the pen of Dean Hook, who observes that, "humanly speaking, it is
scarcely possible to see how, except through the intervention of monasteries,
Christianity, or civilization itself, could have been sustained or handed down
to posterity."—P. 16, vol. ii, *Lives of the Archbishops.*

[2] Fuller states that at one period "Ford Abbey had more learning therein
than three convents of the same size anywhere in England."—*Worthies,* vol. i,
p. 289.

[3] Dr. Hook has thrown a doubt on the generally received opinion on this
point, and suggests that, from the name, he may have been connected with the
family of the founder of Ford Abbey (Richard, son of Baldwin de Brioniis,
sometimes called Richard Fitz-Baldwin), and remarks that "one branch of the
family might easily, in those days, have sunk from wealth to poverty" (p. 542,
vol. ii). When, however, we consider how great a man this Richard Fitz-
Baldwin was; that he had, as we are told, "custodiam totius comitatus Devo-
niæ"; and further, that his mother was niece to the Conqueror,—it seems probable that some tradition at least of Abbot Baldwin's connexion with so illustrious a family would have been preserved; more especially as he was born
only about twenty years after the death of this Richard Fitz-Baldwin.
When archbishop, Baldwin crowned Richard I at Westminster (3rd Sept. 1189),
and afterwards accompanied this monarch to the Holy Land, and died there.

steps to the abbacy of Ford, and thence to the archbishopric
of Canterbury, signally to adorn this his high office), is nevertheless possessed of considerable interest, more particularly
as relates to his own county and the sphere in which he
moved as Abbot, at an eventful period, of one of its most
magnificent and important monasteries.

We are informed by numerous writers that Thomas Chard,
D.D., Suffragan Bishop, and the last Abbot of Ford Abbey,
was born at Tracy's Hays (now known as Tracy), in the
parish of Awliscombe, near Honiton, Devonshire. Sir William
Pole, the great antiquary of Devon, tells us that Tracy was
originally part of the adjoining ancient manor of Ivedon,
which had been held from the Conquest by a family of the
same name, the last of whom, William de Ivedon, divided
the estate (about A.D. 1200) between his three daughters,
his heirs, married respectively to Robert de Stanton,[1] Richard
de Membiry,[2] and William Tracy.[3]   On receiving that portion of the estate that fell to him in dowry, we learn from
the same author that " Tracy called his part Tracyeshayes ;
and soe by Mabbe it descended to Tho. Chard, sonne of Alis,
daughter of Roger Mabb, and contyneweth (about A.D. 1606)
in the issue of Chard"; whilst Prince informs us more speci-
fically that the "Tho. Charde" here alluded to was the father
or grandfather of the abbot of whom we are speaking.[4]   It
must have been about the year A.D. 1470 that this eminent
man was born at Tracy aforesaid.   Of his early years we
know but little, but his subsequent career affords the best
evidence of the care and attention bestowed upon him in
his youth ; and we may judge that his family were of good

---

[1] Stanton's share retained the name of Ivedon ; and we learn that it passed
again by marriage, " so early as anno 27 of King Henry III" (1243) to the
family of Franceis of Franceis Court in this county, who subsequently acquired
also the portion of Membiry by purchase.

[2] Sir William Pole tells us that he was himself descended from the Membiry
branch of the Ivedon family,—a fact that would tend to lend peculiar value to
his testimony respecting them.   In his account of Ivedon he says : " Walter de
la Pole, my auncestor, maried the heire of Membiry, from whom it descended
to Thomas : and John Pole his sonne, sold his part to John Franceis thelder"
(*Collections towards a Description of the County of Devon*, p. 214); thus merg-
ing it again, as we have just stated above in the Stanton branch.

[3] Sir William Pole gives his arms, " Tracy of Ivedon, *argent*, three saltires
sable" ; and Lysons states that " the Traceys possessed an estate in Ivedon so
early as the reign of Richard the First."

[4] *Worthies of Devon*, p. 195.   Chapter on " Chard, Thomas, Doctor of Divinity."

repute and standing in this locality,* both from the circumstance of his ancestor having married the heiress of Tracy, and also from the lengthened period (about four hundred years) during which they afterwards held the estate in unbroken possession in their own name. And here it may be well to observe that though it is chiefly in relation to his office as Abbot, such notices as we have of Dr. Chard have been handed down to us, yet it will be seen as we proceed that he claims our regard also in numerous other important aspects ; and of these more particularly as Suffragan Bishop, which sacred function he zealously discharged during a considerable part of two prelacies.

We gather from various sources that Thomas Chard received the chief part of his. education in the university of Oxford ; and we are told that he entered early at St. Bernard's (now St. John's College), followed his studies with much diligence, and having taken his degrees in arts, quitted Oxford, and retired again to a country life in his own county. Here, devoting his time to the culture of learning and religion, he was led before long to enter on the monastic life ; and having become a monk of the Cistercian order, in the abbey of Ford (of which celebrated monastery he afterwards became Abbot), he, in the years A.D. 1505 and 1507, proceeded to take his degrees respectively as bachelor and doctor of divinity at Oxford ; being recorded, as we are informed in the public register of the time, as a man illustrious for his great learning and virtue,—" vir magnâ doctrinâ et virtute clarus,"—no mean encomium at a time when Oxford stood so pre-eminent for learning.

Notwithstanding, however, this public testimony to his erudition, it is to be regretted, as Prince observes, that he " left no writings behind him, or none that became public"; so that, as regards the particular department in which his learning chiefly displayed itself, we are left in uncertainty. That he was possessed, however, of a very refined and cultivated taste, is attested even at the present day by numerous

* The name occurs also in the adjoining county of Dorset about the same period. Robert Chard was prior of St. John the Baptist, Bridport, in 1534 ; John Chard, brother probably of Robert, was incumbent of the hospital of St. John the Baptist, in the same place, in the year 1553 ; and in his *Notitia Parliamentaria*, Browne Willis tells us a Thomas Chard was returned to parliament, as member for Bridport, in the year 1555. There can be little question that a relationship subsisted between these and the family of the Abbot.

and lasting proofs, which serve at the same time as monuments of his munificence and piety; and in reference to which Prince, with his usual quaintness of style, bears the following testimony : "But for his virtue, that was signally diffusive, especially that kind thereof which consisteth in works of piety and charity,—the memorial of which hath descended to posterity in many particular instances (though some are undoubtedly buried in oblivion) with a fragrant odor home to this day." Of the particular instances of his generosity which the ravages of time, and still more of human faction and discord, have suffered to descend to us, there are none now known to be remaining except those to be found within his own county; which, though it naturally partook most largely of his liberality, must yet by no means be supposed to have set a limit to that "signally diffusive" spirit of charity which appears to have been so distinctive and characteristic a feature of his disposition. We accordingly find that he was no less mindful of the source whence he had drawn his mental than his bodily nurture, and that whilst his name is connected with the endowment of a hospital in the immediate vicinity of his birthplace, it stands gratefully associated also with his college at Oxford; to which, we are told, he became a considerable benefactor, either by repairing the old, or by adding new buildings; and Wood tells us that "his memory was there preserved, as a token of it, in several of the glass windows of that house, particularly in a middle chamber window on the south side of the tower over the common gate of that college (now St. John's); where was, if not still, his name contracted in golden letters (as the fashion was lately on coaches) on an escocheon *sable*, and hath behind it, palewise, an abbat's crozier."[1] These relics, designed to preserve his memory, and so much in keeping with the pious feeling that prompted his restoration of the decaying fabric of his college, Wood, as we have just seen, appears to intimate may have been in existence in his time (1690), though it seems rather probable that they perished in the general and indiscriminate work of spoliation and destruction which was everywhere enacted in the name, and under the sanction, of the Reformation. However this may be, it is certain that all trace of these memorials has now perished, as they were sought for

[1] Fasti Oxonienses, p. 654.

B

some years since with much care and assiduity, but without success.

Having obtained his degrees, he quitted the scene of his early tuition, and returned again to his own county, where his conspicuous talents, which were wholly devoted to the service of religion, speedily secured for him the favourable regard of Dr. Hugh Oldham, then bishop of Exeter; of whom we learn from John Hooker,[1] that, "though he were no great scholar himself, yet was he a great favourer of learning and learned men." Within a year of the time of his taking his doctor's degree, we find Dr. Chard honoured with the highest dignity and mark of confidence his bishop could bestow,—that of selecting him as his own coadjutor in the episcopal office, a step soon followed by his appointment to numerous other important preferments.

Before, however, proceeding to notice more at length the career of distinction which was now about to open upon him, it seems desirable here to correct an error which has gained circulation from its having received the sanction of Wood, and having been subsequently adopted from him by Prince. I refer to the circumstance that these writers allude to two persons, each bearing the name of Thomas Chard, and both flourishing at the same time in the immediate vicinity of each other,—the one said by them to be a *Benedictine*, who was bishop of Solubria and prior of Montacute; the other a *Cistercian*, and the abbot of Ford Abbey. There can now be no doubt that those who have been thus treated of as two distinct persons, were in reality one and the same individual,—the Thomas Chard of whom we are here speaking. Dugdale, Cleaveland, Risdon, Lysons, Oliver, and many other authorities on the subject, make no allusion

---

[1] "Catalog of the Bishops of Excester, with the Description of the Antiquitie and first Foundation of the Cathedrall Church of the same. Collected by John Vowell *alias* Hoker, Gentleman. Lond., 4to., 1584." We learn also from this source that it was to the suggestion of Bishop Oldham that we are indebted for Corpus Christi College at Oxford, which Bishop Fox intended for a monastery; but was induced by his friend Oldham, who also contributed the large sum of six thousand marks towards its foundation, to convert it into a seminary for learning. Oldham seems further to have been associated with Bishop Fox in founding the Grammar School at Taunton. In his *History of Taunton* (1791), Toulmin states, in describing the Grammar School, "Above the entrance are the arms of that bishop (Fox), *azure*, a pelican *or*, feeding her young; and the arms of Hugh Oldham, bishop of Exeter,—*sable*, a chevron, *or*, between three owls prr.; on a chief of the second, as many roses *gules*."—P. 33. The arms of Oldham have since this been removed, but those of Bishop Fox still remain.

whatever to any second person of this name; whilst on the other hand several of them concur in speaking of the Thomas Chard who was born at Tracy, as being at the same time the last abbot of Ford Abbey and also suffragan to Bishop Oldham,—a fact which is, indeed, proved by the actual existence of monuments indubitably attesting it even at the present day. What may have been the cause originally suggestive of the confusion just alluded to, it is now by no means easy to discover; the only one that presents itself as affording any ground for it, so far as I can ascertain, being, that amongst his other preferments Thomas Chard for a time held the priorship of the *Benedictine* monastery of Montacute in Somerset,—a fact which, it must be presumed, may have been regarded as irreconcilable with his being at the same time of the *Cistercian* order, as evidenced by his having entered at St. Bernard's College, Oxford; and his having professed in, and subsequently become superior of, so noted a Cistercian community as that of the "monastery of Foord" in Devonshire. On this point, however, and with a view of setting the question finally at rest, I may perhaps be permitted to refer to a portion of a letter, dated Exeter, 21st January, 1859, which the late Rev. Dr. Oliver, admittedly the highest authority on all questions of this nature, relating to the county of Devon, did me the favour to address to me on the subject. In reply to an inquiry on my part he says :

"Let me begin by expressing my *unbelief* that Thomas Chard, the abbot of Ford Abbey, and Thomas Chard, prior of Montacute, were distinct persons. From all quarters pluralities were heaped upon Thomas Chard, bishop of Solubria *in partibus infidelium*, the coadjutor or suffragan of Bishop Oldham, the bishop of Exeter, to support his honourable station ; in the same way as Cardinal Wolsey was allowed to hold *in commendam* the abbot's rank in St. Alban's monastery, and the bishopric of Winchester on the death of Richard Fox. The duties of superiority could be exercised by deputy. You are aware also that in the nine cathedrals in this country, which were served by a community of Benedictine monks, viz. Bath, Canterbury, Coventry, Durham, Ely, Norwich, Rochester, Winchester, and Worcester, their bishops, whether members of the secular clergy, or of any religious order, Franciscan, Dominican, etc., always ranked as abbots of those Benedictine communities."

After this explanation of the only point of apparent discrepancy which could have afforded ground for the mistake,

and with the high authority of Dr. Oliver thus decidedly
expressed on the subject,—possessed, too, as he was of the
advantage of all previously existing information upon it,—
this question may, we think, be safely dismissed from further
discussion; more especially as we shall see, when we come
to describe Ford Abbey, that the three shields on the front
entrance tower, with other similar evidences, still remain,—
an indisputable proof of the fact that Thomas Chard united
in his own person the offices of suffragan bishop and abbot
of Ford Abbey.

Quitting this topic, however, it would seem well to bestow
a few words on another point bearing, in respect of ambi-
guity, some similarity to it, viz., that we sometimes find the
last abbot of Ford styled Thomas Chard *alias* Tybbes. The
usage of thus employing an *alias*[1] was very prevalent at the
period at which he lived, and was adopted even by indivi-
duals themselves. Thus we find a contemporary and noted
countryman of his, John Hooker, Chamberlain of Exeter,
born in 1521, author of many valuable works (and uncle to
the celebrated Richard Hooker), is frequently styled John
Hooker *alias* Vowel; and we are told[2] that "in early life he
used to sign himself John Vowel *alias* Hooker, but in later
years John Hooker *alias* Vowel." In the instance of the
last abbot of Ford there is little doubt but that his mother's
maiden name was Tybbes; that Chard was his paternal
name is certain, not only from the concurrent testimony of
every writer who makes mention of him, but also from the
name, Thomas Chard, being thus entered in the register of
his college at Oxford, and subsequently preserved, as we
have before noticed, "in several of the glass windows of
that house"; from its actual existence still in full over the
entrance tower, with the initials T. C. on shields, etc., on
various other parts of Ford Abbey; from his vesting the
patronage of the leper hospital at Honiton, together with a
yearly head-rent attached to it, in the heir male of this
family of Chard, living at Tracy, his birth-place; from his
will, which until lately was in the Prerogative Court of Can-

---

[1] Bishop Veysey, to whom also Dr. Chard was suffragan, was styled Veysey
alias Harman, having acquired the name of Veysey for no other reason, as
Wood tells us, than "because he was educated in his infancy, as 'tis said, by
one of that name."—*Athen. Oxon.*, p. 581.

[2] Hooker's Works, by Keble. Oxford, 1845.

terbury in that name;[1] as well likewise as from tradition in the family of the writer of these pages, who still holds deeds and other objects relating to the family of Chard in his possession,—an ancestor of his having, in 1690, married Mary Chard of Tracy, of the same family, then still residing in the same house at Tracy in which the abbot was born.

Having digressed thus much in order to dispose of these two questions, which, if allowed to remain unnoticed, might still continue to prove a source of confusion, I proceed to consider in detail some of the more important offices which, during the course of a long and useful life, were discharged by this eminent ecclesiastic. It was in the early part of the year 1508, soon after he took his doctor's degree, that, as suffragan to Bishop Oldham, he was promoted to the episcopacy under the title of "Episcopus Solubricensis"; which sacred office he continued to exercise during the life of Oldham, and for some years afterwards with his successor, Bishop Veysey. With a view to the proper maintenance of his episcopal dignity, we find numerous preferments were bestowed upon Dr. Chard; and the rapidity with which they were multiplied may be regarded as the best evidence of his conscientious and successful discharge of the duties successively attaching to them, more particularly as we observe him frequently resigning such as he found himself unequal to attend to with due satisfaction to himself.

Soon after his consecration (26th Sept. 1508) he was collated by Bishop Oldham to the living of Torrington Parva, and was likewise preferred to St. Gluvias in Cornwall; which latter, however, he resigned some years after. In June 1512, on the resignation of Dr. Richard Gilbert, he was collated to the vicarage of Wellington in Somerset, in the ancient church of which we may picture him to ourselves officiating before the altar, having at its back the elaborate and gorgeous reredos, then standing in full splendour and preservation, and which has been so ably described by Mr. Giles;[2] and is now to be seen, a mere relic of antiquarian curiosity, in the Museum at Taunton. On the 9th October, 1513, he was appointed to the wardenship of the College of Ottery St. Mary, Devon, which he resigned about three

---

[1] Athen. Oxon., p.576. Note (a) in Reg. Pynning in Offic. Prærog. Cant., Qu. 17.
[2] Proceedings of the Somersetshire Archæological and Natural History Society, vol. i, p. 30.

years subsequently, to be instituted to the vicarage of Holbeton in the deanery of Totnes. . In the year 1515 he was
chosen prior of Montacute, a monastery of the Cluniac or
Benedictine order in the county of Somerset; being at the
same time elected also to the priorship of Carswell, a small
priory dependent upon Montacute, but situated in the
deanery of Plymtree, Devon. The former of these he resigned
in 1525, but the latter he retained until its dissolution. On
the 24th October, 1520, he resigned the living of Holbeton;
reserving, however, an annuity of 12l. a year from its profits;
and in August of the following year he was instituted to
the vicarage of Tintinhull, in the diocese of Bath and Wells,
Somerset. It was in this year also, although an earlier
period has been assigned by some, that he succeeded to the
abbacy. Wood, in noting the time of his taking his degrees,
speaks of him in his *Fasti* as " the Ven^ble Father Thomas
Chard, a monk of the Cistercian order, and abbat of the
monastery of Foord in Devonshire"; but this is a form of
designation which would naturally be adopted, writing of
him, as Wood does, nearly two hundred years after the
time he flourished, yet without by any means intending to
imply that he was abbot of Ford at the time he took his
degrees. It is this circumstance, however, which has led
Prince and others to conclude that he was abbot when he
took his bachelor's degree in 1505, though we have abundant
proof to the contrary; of which it may be sufficient here to
mention that his predecessor, Abbot Whyte, did not die until
the year 1521; and so late as the 18th of April of that year
he granted to Richard Hayball, his wife Jane, and their son
William, a lease of the manor house of Sadborow, with
various lands, fields, etc.

After this, on the 15th April, 1529, Bishop Veysey instituted Dr. Chard to the vicarage of Thorncombe, the parish
in which his abbey was situated; and on the 10th April,
1532, to the rectory of Northyll, in the archdeaconry of
Cornwall. The last preferment we find him recorded as
having received, was that to the office of minister of the
College at Ottery St. Mary, of which he had previously held
the wardenship. He was appointed minister on 22nd March,
1540; and resigned the office again, in about three years
time, just before his death, which happened in the early
part of the year 1544.

In thus recounting this lengthened catalogue of Dr. Chard's preferments, there are those who may perhaps feel disposed to make it rather an occasion of cavil, and endeavour to represent it as furnishing evidence of little else than a spirit of cupidity. So far, however, as there are now any means of ascertaining the truth, there appears no reason whatever for entertaining so ungenerous a suspicion, and one so utterly at variance with the testimony which all writers have given of his general character: indeed, a sufficient refutation of any such idea is furnished not only by the evidence afforded by his many other charitable acts, but also by the fact that, of the numerous benefices he held, many are still recorded as having borne some lasting impress of his bounty.

In passing, then, from this enumeration of the offices he filled, we shall now proceed to advert to some of the more remarkable incidents of Dr. Chard's life, especially those we find recorded in connexion with the discharge of the duties the more important of his numerous appointments entailed upon him. We shall therefore notice him first in his office of suffragan bishop, and then in his character as abbot of Ford Abbey. I am indebted to a private letter from the late Dr. Oliver for the information that, at the end of Bishop Oldham's *Register* are given the several dates of Dr. Chard's holding ordinations as suffragan, " vice et auctoritate" of his ordinary, Hugh Oldham, Lord Bishop of Exeter. It was on Saturday of the Ember week (the 23rd September), 1508, in the first year of his consecration (" consecrationis suæ anno primo") that the Rev. Father Thomas, Bishop of Solubria, first administered holy orders in St. Mary's Chapel within the palace of Exeter. Again, on the 27th September in the following year, 1509, he gave ordinations in the church of the Dominican Convent, Exeter. On the 6th September, 1516, we read that he held a considerable ordination in the chapel of St. Katherine's Almshouse, Exeter (" in capella Sancte Catherine infra domum elemosinarium juxta clausum ecclesiæ cathedralis Exon"); and it appears he performed this office of conferring orders for the said diocesan bishop in all thirty-eight times. For his successor, John Veysey, he administered holy orders about thirty-four times. The last ordination he held for this lord bishop of Exeter was on the 20th September, 1532, " in ecclesia sive capella domus aut prioratus de Karswell," in Broad-

hembury parish; soon after which he must have resigned
the coadjutorship, as we find that William Collumpton, the
last prior of St. Nicholas, Exeter, was shortly after consecrated bishop of Hippo; and as coadjutor to Bishop Veysey
held his first ordination in the Lady Chapel of the cathe-
dral on 21st December, 1532.   It was during the period of
Dr. Chard's suffraganship that such considerable alterations
and additions were made in the church of St. Petrock,
Exeter, as rendered it expedient it should be consecrated
afresh,—a duty which devolved on him; and we accordingly
find that, on 22nd July, 1513, Thomas Chard, suffragan of
Bishop Oldham, consecrated, dedicated, and blessed the
church ("Thomas, Episcopus Salubriæ, consecravit, dedica-
vit, et benedixit ecclesiam S'c'i Petroci, Exon").[1]   On the
21st August, 1523, a commission was directed to Thomas
Chard, as suffragan to Bishop Veysey, for his benediction of
Simon Rede, who had just been elected and confirmed abbot
of Tor Abbey.[2]   There is only one other instance in which
I have met with his name as associated with the discharge
of his episcopal office.   I allude to his having officiated as
suffragan, in place of his bishop, at the noted funeral of
Katherine de Courtenay, widow of William Courtenay, Earl
of Devon, and daughter of King Edward IV.   This illustrious lady died at her residence, the Castle of Tiverton, on
Friday, 15th Nov., 1527; and her funeral obsequies were
performed with more than usual solemnity and state, Nor-
roy King of Arms and Richmond Herald-at-Arms being sent
down from London, we are told, expressly to conduct the
ceremony; of which a very full and interesting account is
given by Col. Harding in his *History of Tiverton*, though
he has fallen into the mistake of speaking of the lord suffragan and the abbot of Ford as two distinct persons.
    We learn that the body of the princess, having been
embalmed, cered, leaded, and chested, was conveyed to the
chapel belonging to the Castle, and placed within a bar; the
coffin being covered with a pall of black velvet having a
cross of white satin, and upon that another pall of cloth of
gold with a white cross of silver tissue, garnished with six
escutcheons of her arms.   The corpse was attended day and
night until Monday the 2nd December, when, in formal procession, it was brought to St. Peter's Church, under a canopy

---

[1] Oldham's *Reg.*   [2] Oliver's *Monasticon*, p. 17.

of black velvet borne by six esquires ; and the coffin was carried by six tall yeomen, attended by Sir Thomas Dennys, Sir John Bassett, Sir William Carew, and Philip Champernon, Esq. At each corner, bearing a banner of a saint (viz. of the Trinity, our Lady, St. Edward, and St. Catherine), walked George Carew, Nicholas Ashford, Richard Chudleigh, and Alexander Wood, Esquires, all in black gowns and hoods. The chief mourner was Lady Carew, assisted by Sir Piers Edgcombe; and her train was borne by a gentleman followed by six ladies. The body was received at the church by the Lord Suffragan, abbot of Ford, and by the abbot of Tor, who sprinkled the coffin with holy water. The funeral was also attended by many other persons of high ecclesiastical rank, who, with the abbots and a hundred gentlemen, had preceded the corpse in the procession, following in the order of their rank. The coffin was placed in the chapel belonging to the family, covered with a rich pall of cloth of gold tissue, upon which was a cross of silver, whilst four lights of virgin wax displayed the splendour of the whole. A dirge having been sung, and other funeral ceremonies performed, the company returned in the same order to the castle, where they partook of refreshments which had been prepared for them. The body lay in state, watched by attendants the whole night. The following morning, at seven, the company proceeded to the church in the same solemn procession, and the mass of Requiem was sung by the Lord Suffragan (who acted as principal on the mournful occasion), in which he was assisted by the most eminent choristers from Exeter, as well as from every part of the county. Offerings were then made by all the persons present, in the order of their rank, beginning with the chief mourner, whose contribution was 6s. 8d.; the knights and gentlemen, the mayor and aldermen of Exeter, the yeomen, and other attendants, gave in proportion. Dr. Sarsley preached from the words "Manus Domini tetigit me." When he had concluded, and the service finished, the body was let down into a vault, on which the officers of the deceased princess broke their staves. The Lord Suffragan, with all the other abbots and prelates, returned in their pontificals to the Castle, where they partook of a splendid entertainment; provision being made for five hundred persons; and a dole of one hundred marks was divided to eight thousand poor people (two pence to each), to pray for the soul of the deceased princess.

I have availed myself of the foregoing account, taken chiefly from the *History of Tiverton* already alluded to, as it affords us a curious insight into the customs of the times, brings before us many eminent names still familiar in Devonshire, and exhibits specially to our view the Subject of this Memoir taking an active and most conspicuous part in the very interesting ceremony which it describes.

In passing now to a consideration of Dr. Chard's character as Abbot, it becomes desirable, in the first place, to offer some description of his abbey,—that object which naturally claimed so large a share of his regard, with which his memory is more intimately associated than any other, and which has repaid the care he bestowed upon it, in so far as it still remains a monument of his piety, and one of the chief features of architectural beauty and antiquarian interest in the county which it adorns.   Various other authorities concur with Camden in informing us that Ford Abbey was founded in the year 1140, for Cistercian monks, by Adelize, daughter of Baldwine of Oakhampton, and grand-niece to William the Conqueror. The circumstances of the migration, in 1136, of twelve monks, with their abbot, from Waverley in Surrey, to Brightley within the honour of Oakhampton, Devon, and the romantic story connected with their removal from this latter place to Ford, may be found fully detailed in any of the numerous accounts which have been given of the abbey, and more particularly in a *History of Ford Abbey*, published anonymously in the year 1846. The site selected for the erection of the abbey was in the valley, on the left bank of the river Axe, at an extreme outlying point of the county of Devon, called at that period, as we learn from Leland, Hertbath (*balneum cervorum*),—not Hartescath, as we commonly find it written,—and which, from its contiguity to a ford at this part of the river, subsequently acquired the name of Ford. Here then, by the pious care of Adelicia, was laid, in this fertile and sequestered spot, the foundation of that splendid pile of building which still commands our admiration and interest; though, excepting some portion of what is known under the designation of "the Chapel," at the eastern end of the south front, nothing now remains of the original structure.   In this, however, which is termed "the Chapel," are still to be seen considerable vestiges which sufficiently attest its Norman origin, and which we may legiti-

mately assume arose under the immediate auspices, and very
probably under the actual superintendence, of the grand-
niece of the Conqueror himself. On inspecting its eastern
end, on the exterior, the quoins will at once be observed to
exhibit the marked characteristics of the Norman style;
whilst the window which has been introduced between them
is obviously of the period of Dr. Chard; and that it was
inserted by him is manifest from the panel with the stag's
head, which may be seen on the left hand side, at the upper
part of the window; whilst parallel to it, though almost
hidden by ivy, may be discerned traces of the companion
panel, containing doubtless the oft-repeated monogram of
T. C.

On passing from this to the interior we further meet with
some fine specimens of Anglo-Norman work, in the pillars,
the groined stone roof and arches at each end, slightly
pointed and ornamented with chevron mouldings; though
even here the portions that remain bear evidences of muti-
lation, and are partially obscured by a pulpit, with panelled
wood-work round the walls, erected apparently for the purpose of giving it the character of a chapel.

On the question of the original purpose of this ancient
portion of the building there exists, however, some difference
of opinion. In his latest notice of it, in the supplement to
his *Monasticon*, Dr. Oliver speaks of it as the Chapter House;
and my friend, the Rev. F. Warre, with whom I had the
advantage of visiting the abbey last year, at once expressed
himself to the same effect, though without the slightest knowledge, I apprehend, of the views entertained by Dr. Oliver.
On the other hand, it has been more commonly regarded as
the Chapel; and in this light it has frequently been referred
to as the resting-place of the mortal remains of the Lady
Adelicia, the foundress, of several of the Courtenays, and of
other benefactors to the abbey. Without committing myself
to an opinion on a point I do not feel competent to decide,
I would venture to observe that there does not appear to be
sufficient ground for the conclusion that it ever formed the
burying-place of the early benefactors to the abbey before
alluded to; but it seems much more probable that they were
buried in the conventual church itself, the place of sepulture
to which, as is well known, preference was most commonly
given at that period. It is strange, however, that except in

the deed of surrender, and a short reference made to it by
Hearne, I have not been able to discover the slightest notice
of "the Church of the Blessed Virgin Mary of Ford" in any
of the numerous accounts which have been given of the
abbey; though, when we read of frequent interments, some
on the north, others on the south side of the choir,—others,
such as that of Robert Courtenay, who, we are told, was
buried on the 28th July, 1242, in the chancel, before the
high altar, under a stately monument[1] exhibiting the figure
of an armed knight,—there can be little doubt, I think, that
these took place, not in what is now known as the Chapel,
but in the Abbey Church, which stood at the east end of the
abbey, about two hundred feet above the Chapel. As the
notice of the church by Hearne is the fullest I have met
with, and as it has not appeared, so far as I am aware, in
any of the previous accounts which have been given of the
abbey, I am the more readily induced to insert it here.
Writing of Godstowe Abbey, and describing its chapel,
Hearne says : "This was a private chapel for the nuns, the
church being used on public occasions; as there were private
chapells in many other religious houses, one whereof (to
instance no more) is now to be seen in the eastermost end
of Ford Abbey before mentioned, and is made use of as the
family chapell ; the Abbey Church itself, which stood at the
east end of the said south front, about two hundred feet
above the Chapel (commonly called *the Oratory*), being so
entirely demolished that the oldest man now living in those
parts (as I am assured by a very ingenious friend) does not
remember to have seen any part of it standing, though in
making the gardens they often dig up human bones."[2]

Next in point of antiquarian interest, or at least in point
of antiquity to the Chapel, is what is now termed the Monk's
Walk; a range of ivy-clad buildings nearly four hundred
feet in length, and running back from the eastern end of the
abbey in a northerly direction; whilst a similar range, most
probably, ran parallel to it, extending from the western end
of the abbey.   The wing still remaining on the eastern side

[1] In the form of a pyramid, about which was written the following epitaph :
   " Hic jacet ingenui de Courtenay gleba Roberti
   Militis egregii virtutum laude referti
   Quem genuit strenuus Reginaldus Courtiniensis
   Qui procer Eximius fuerat tunc Devoniensis."
[2] Note to the third volume *Gulielmi Neubrigensis*, p. 778.

consists of two storeys, the lower of which contains some beautiful Early English work, and forms, as it were, a continuation of the ancient cloisters; whilst the upper was evidently the ancient dormitory. This wing, still retaining the name of the Monk's Walk, presents in its centre a good archway of the fourteenth century, with a series of lancet-shaped windows extending throughout its entire length, and still quite perfect on its western side; though on the eastern side they appear to have been fewer in number, and even of these many have been walled up and destroyed. We find a notice of this wing of the abbey also by Hearne, by whom it is thus described : "But now, though one of the chief uses of the cloysters was for walking, yet in Religious Houses they had sometime galleries for the same end. We have an instance of it in Ford Abbey in Devonshire, which is one of the most entire abbeys in England; in the east front whereof, which is the oldest of the two fronts (though the south front be the chiefest), there is a gallery called the Monk's Walk, with small cells on the right hand, and little narrow windows on the left."

As an instance of the loose manner in which the materials for county history are occasionally put together, it may be remarked that it is only from the notice conveyed in this passage that Lysons is content to draw all his information respecting this wing of the abbey; which, from his manner of speaking of it, one might be led rather to suppose was no longer in existence. He says : "It appears by a note of Thomas Hearne's, that about a century ago there remained a gallery called the Monk's Walk, with small, narrow windows and the cells of the monks"; thus merely alluding to it as a thing of the past,—which "about a century ago remained there,"—and affording the reader no ground to conclude that the Monk's Walk may still be seen apparently as perfect as when referred to by Hearne.

We now come to speak of the main body of this noble fabric, which almost in its entire extent is the work of Dr. Chard. It is only on passing to the front of the abbey itself that a just idea of its grandeur is obtained. Here nearly all that meets the view is the work of the Last Abbot, and affords a striking instance of his consummate taste and devoted perseverance under circumstances that may well have discouraged him from the enterprise; for, as has been observed, there can be no doubt he foresaw the storm that was impending over the Church; but instead of suffering the threatening danger to strike him with dismay, or to paralyse his efforts, it led him rather, we are told, " to set his house in order," possibly in the hope that its very beauty might serve as an appeal to stay the hands of its spoilers; and that thus, as has actually happened, it might survive the common wreck in which nearly all similar edifices throughout the land were about to be ruthlessly involved. And here, as it will be necessary to enter on a more detailed description of this portion of the building, I shall not hesitate to avail myself, to a considerable extent, of the accounts which already exist; and more particularly of that which, though published anonymously, is known to have been furnished by one who for a long period enjoyed the advantage of a residence in the abbey, and was thus enabled to form a more familiar and exact acquaintance with its minute architectural details than could possibly be obtained by any one who, like the writer of these pages, had only such opportunity for a hasty visit as a day snatched from the ordinary avocations of professional life might suffice to afford. Speaking of the abbey as it now is, we read in the *History of Ford Abbey*,—

"The mansion is approached from Chard by a bridge over the Axe; and on entering the carriage-drive the eastern portion, or Monk's Walk side of the house is presented to view, covered with luxuriant ivy, the growth of centuries. A feeling of disappointment is here felt at its appearance ; and it is not until by ascending a gentle acclivity to the south of the Chapel that the magnificent front bursts on the sight in unparalleled beauty, filling the beholder with admiration and delight. The portions still remaining, built by Dr. Thomas Chard (the last abbot) now appear to advantage. The first claiming attention is the cloister, in the florid Gothic or Tudor style ; the mullions and tracery of the windows beautifully designed ; and over them a frieze of stonework, with the shields of the arms of various benefactors to the abbey, viz., the Courtenays quartering Rivers ; those of Poulett, the bishop of Exeter, etc.; and T. C., the initials of Thomas Chard"; whilst on some of these shields the name " Tho. Chard" occurs at full length, as may be observed in a portion of the frieze, of which a sketch is here given. "It is strange that neither the arms of the abbey nor of Dr. Chard appear on this or any other part of the building....Edmondson tells us that the Chard arms are, *or* and *gules* quarterly, over all a label of

✠ A PORTION OF THE FRIEZE AND WINDOW OF THE CLOISTER:
FORD ABBEY: THE WORK OF ABBAT CHARD. AD 1528.

fivo points; *az.*; and a learned friend has informed us that he has seen the same on an old deed belonging to that family."[1]

" The cloister is divided by a suite of rooms and arcade from the grand porch-tower, so conspicuous for its architectural beauty, and which in days gone by was no doubt the original entrance." (See the drawing of the porch-tower inserted as a frontispiece.) " It is richly ornamented with first-rate sculpture, some of it obviously unfinished ; the central boss in the vaulting uncut; and the blank shield in the centre, below the basement window, encircled by the garter, was doubt-less intended for the royal arms. The uncut shield on the sinister side, having the pelican and dolphin for supporters, was for Couttenay. The two small shields cut are charged with a lion rampant for De Redvers, and checky two bars for Baldwin de Brioniis. Immediately over the arch of the door is a large scroll shield of a more modern date, bearing the arms of Prideaux; impaling those of his second wife, Ivery. On the upper part of this elegant specimen of Dr. Chard's taste, in the centre shield, are his initials, T. C., with the crosier and *mitre* (Dr. Chard was suffragan bishop) ; and the two smaller shields with the T. C., crosier, and abbot's cap, alternate with the stag's head cabossed, —supposed to be the bearing of the then bishop of Exeter ;[2] and just below the battlement of the tower is the following inscription :

𝔄𝔫'𝔬 𝔇'𝔫𝔦 𝔪𝔦𝔩𝔩𝔢𝔰𝔦𝔪𝔬 𝔮𝔲𝔦𝔫𝔤𝔢𝔰𝔦𝔪𝔬 𝔟𝔦𝔠ᵐᵒ 𝔬𝔠𝔱𝔬°. 𝔄 𝔇'𝔫𝔬 𝔣𝔞𝔠𝔱𝔲𝔪 𝔢𝔰𝔱 𝔗𝔥𝔬𝔪𝔞 𝔠𝔥𝔞𝔯𝔡, 𝔞𝔟𝔟.

It is presumed that stronger evidence than that furnished by the three shields thus commented on by the writer can scarcely be needed to prove that Dr. Chard united in his own person the offices of Abbot and Suffragan Bishop; and yet, as if still further to prevent the possibility of mistake on the point, there is a remarkable panel in the frieze over the cloisters, which appears to have been designed to attest the

[1] I have in my possession an ancient hatchment removed some years since from the north or Tracy aisle of Awliscombe Church, in which the Chard arms, *or* and *gules* quarterly, are impaled with those of the now likewise extinct family of Reigny of Culm Reigny, Brixton Reigny, etc.,—*gules*, three paring knives *argent*, hafts *or*.

[2] This is a manifest mistake. The stag's head cabossed, with a crosier pass-ing through it palewise, was neither the arms of Bishop Oldham nor of his successor Veysey. It has been suggested by the Rev. F. Warre that it is very probably the ancient cognizance of the Abbey, connected with the earliest name of the site on which it stood, which we have already seen was Hertbath (*balneum cervorum*). In a letter from the Last Abbot of Ford to Cardinal Wolsey (a copy of which will be found at a subsequent page), it will be observed that the stag's head cabossed is used as the seal, and is expressly referred to in the body of the letter by Dr. Chard as "*sigillum meum.*" We find it also almost uniformly associated with his initials or name in the numerous instances in which it occurs on various parts of the abbey buildings.

fact as clearly as if it had been expressed in so many words. A drawing of this panel is here given, and it will at once be seen that it contains within itself all the evidence that could be accumulated in proof of the fact it is manifestly intended to record. The letters T. C., with the abbot's and bishop's crosiers, will be observed in the small corner shields; whilst in the larger one, which occupies the centre, occur the stag's head and crosier, the name "Tho. Chard" on a scroll entwined round a crosier; and above these, as a crowning feature of the whole, the abbot's cap; surmounted, over all, by the bishop's mitre.

"In the entrance porch there is a handsome window to the west, corresponding with those of the adjoining great hall (which are in unison with those of the cloister), and over is a frieze of grotesque animals. This part of the building has been shorn of its length, as, on minute inspection, will appear. The royal arms are not in the centre, as they no doubt originally were. They consist of a rose crowned, encircled with a garter, and supported by a dragon and greyhound, the badges of Henry VII....Although the remaining portion of this wing has been altered, it was built by Thomas Chard, the battlements corresponding with the tower and Chapel; and as a more decisive proof that it was so, there is, at the western end of the building, but hid by ivy, the portcullis cut in stone, another of the badges of Henry VII; and to the north, or back side, are the initials T. C., with the crosier and cap."

The initials, etc., in this instance are encircled by a wreath with an angel on either side, in the kneeling posture, supporting the wreath.

"We will now lead the uninitiated to the interior, where scenes of great beauty await the eye. The entrance on the eastern side is through a vestibule to the cloister, eighty-two feet in length and seventeen feet high; the vaulting and tracery as perfect as when built by Dr. Chard, and in beautiful keeping with its external appearance and workmanship. It is now used as a conservatory, and filled with luxuriant orange and lemon trees. Here we first notice the handiwork of Inigo Jones in the square doors at each end, destroying its harmony. Ascending a flight of steps, we come to two rooms to the left,—first a comfortable dining-parlour, panelled and gilt, and surrounded by some good paintings; secondly, a morning-room having a chaste Grecian ceiling, with three windows facing the lawn, and opening into it, and another to the west, making it airy and cheerful. We now return, and enter the great hall or refectory, fifty-five feet by twenty-seven feet nine

A PANEL IN THE FRIEZE OVER THE CLOISTERS:

FORD ABBEY. CONTAINING BOTH THE ABBAT'S CAP AND BISHOP'S MITRE.

inches; height, twenty-eight feet; having four large windows to the south, answered by blank panels of corresponding design to the north, which in olden time, when Master Tyler 'expounded the Scripture to the brethren,' were in all probability open. The ceiling is flattened, of beautifully carved wainscot, painted and gilt, with gold stars in the compartments."

It seems unnecessary to follow this description further, devoted, as it subsequently is, almost exclusively to a detail of the alteration and adaptation of the interior of the building to suit the purposes of a modern mansion; which, however interesting in itself, has little, if anything, to identify it with the subject of this memoir. As, however, it has not been noticed by the writer of the foregoing account, it may here be observed that, at right angles to the great hall, and now converted into a kitchen and domestic offices, is what was once the ancient guest-chamber, as evidenced in certain places where portions of the modern ceiling have fallen down, disclosing the ancient roof. What may have been the actual condition of the abbey at the time its restoration was undertaken by the Last Abbot, we are unfortunately left without record; but assuming its decay to have been in any degree commensurate in extent with the portions of Dr. Chard's work which at present exist, his undertaking, as may be readily gathered from the foregoing description, must have been little short of a rebuilding of the whole body of the fabric; whilst the character of what has come down to us serves to assure us how generally and entirely applicable was the remark of Leland, who, visiting the abbey during the progress of the work, states—" Cœnobium nunc sumptibus plane non credendis abbas magnificentissime restaurat."

To Mr. Davidson, of Sector near Axminster, we are indebted for the discovery of the abbey seal, which had previously eluded the research of the editors of Dugdale's *Monasticon*. It has since been engraved in Oliver's *Monasticon Diocesis Exoniensis* (first Suppl.), is of an oval form, and divided into three compartments. In the upper part, between two pointed windows, a bell appears suspended in a steeple. In the canopy beneath, is the Blessed Virgin with the Divine Infant on her knee. On the dexter side is the Courtenay shield,—*or*, three torteauxes, with a label of three points. On the sinister, is the shield of Beaumont,—barry of six,

D

vairy and *gules.* In the lower compartment is the abbot erect, holding his crosier in the right hand, and a book in the left; and three persons, apparently monks, on their knees. The legend is—

S': commbne : Monasterii : Beate : Marie : De : Forde.

(See the accompanying figure.)

Reverting for a moment to a consideration of the interior of the abbey, it may be observed that we seek now in vain for the adornings, in neat and fair wainscot, curiously carved, of which Prince makes mention ; nor do I feel at all certain that any such ever existed. Though no one has more richly contributed to the biographical and general history of his county than Prince, it is nevertheless strange that a resident in Devon for eighty years, and born within seven miles of Ford Abbey, he should never have visited this beautiful and interesting relic of antiquity ! That he never saw it for himself, but borrowed his account only from Risdon, may, I think be legitimately inferred from the following passage: "Nor was Dr. Chard a less, he was rather a greater benefactor to his abbey than his college....His adornings thereof, whatever his buildings were, consisted in neat and fair wainscot curiously carved, where the two first letters of his name, T. C., were intermixed, as if he had designed to make himself as immortal as his abbey."[1] The remark, "his adornings thereof, *whatever his buildings were*," seems clearly, I think, to shew that these "buildings" had never been seen by one who could thus write of them; and when we turn to the account given by Risdon, from which Prince has borrowed, and to which he refers us, we find it is as follows :—"This fabric (Ford Abbey), though it have yielded up to time its antique beauty, yet somewhat sheweth of what magnificence once it was; whose structure, stately and high withal, amongst curious carvings sheweth the letters T. C. intermixed, which (some affirm) served for the last abbot's name there, Thomas Charde."[2] Here, then, I think the reference to the "fabric, whose structure, stately and high withal, amongst curious carvings sheweth the letters T. C. intermixed," by no means proves the said carvings to have been, as Prince states, "in neat and fair

[1] P. 190. 4to. edition.
[2] Risdon's *Survey of Devon*, p. 15. (1811), printed from the original MSS. of 1630.

SEAL OF FORD ABBEY.

wainscot"; but rather that they, with the letters T. C. intermixed, were in that more solid and durable material of
which the stately fabric itself is composed; and which we
have seen offers to our view these initial letters, together
with the name Thomas Chard in full; both being still in
existence, and the former especially profusely scattered over
the front, and occasionally over the back of the exterior of
the building.

In the internal administration of the affairs of his convent,
the rule of Abbot Chard was marked by that steady and
consistent discharge of his duty for which his public life
was so conspicuously distinguished.   We read that, for the
period of nearly twenty years during which he presided
over his abbey, "his government was judicious, and his
devotion to his duties great. But his career must have been
an anxious and troublous one. The approaching reformation
was indicated by repeated occurrences which must have
kept him in a state of constant alarm ; whilst the unscrupu-
lous character of the monarch held out little hope of consideration or respect for the ancient faith and its institutions,
should they prove impediments to his kingly purposes.
With reason might the crosier tremble in the grasp from
which it was destined to be speedily and rudely snatched."[1]
In the midst, however, of all the distracting influences incident to this eventful period, we find Dr. Chard attending
with his accustomed devotion to the religious services of his
office, and at the same time bestowing due regard upon the
discharge of its numerous and various temporal duties. We
learn that he engaged the services of William Tyler, M.A.,
of Axminster, to undertake the instruction of boys in the
monastery in grammar, and also to expound the Scriptures
in the refectory when required; and a long list of leases
granted by him evinces his activity in matters more strictly
secular.

The record, moreover, of a transaction highly interesting,
because characteristic of the times, and which introduces
him to our notice soon after his accession to the office, has
very fortunately been preserved, and is still in existence,
with his own signature as Abbot attached. Whilst purport-
ing to be simply an acknowledgment of a debt to Cardinal
Wolsey, the ominously significant nature of the document

---

[1] *The Book of the Axe*, by G. P. R. Pulman. London, 1854.

was doubtless felt in all its force by the Last Abbot, and the
thoughts it would tend to inspire may well account for the
imperfect and unsteady character in which his name is
traced. The original was in the possession of the late
F. G. Coleridge, Esq., of Ottery St. Mary, and has been
printed in the second Supplement (p. 31) to Dr. Oliver's
Monasticon Diocesis Exoniensis. It is as follows :

"Ego Thomas, abbas monasterii beate Virginis Marie de Ffordà,
ordinis Cisterciensis, Sacre Theologie Professor, fateor me debere
Reverendissimo in Christo Patri Dūo Thome Cardinali Eboracensi, nec-
non legato de latere, pro procurationibus variorum monasteriorum dicti
ordinis infra regnum Anglie ciiilͥ. vs. solvendos London predicto Reverendissimo Dūo Cardinali ad tria Festa Paschæ immediate subseqnentia
post datum presentium per equales portiones. In cujus rei testimonium
sigillum meum apposui et manu propriâ subscripsi. Datum anno Dūi
millesimo quingentessimo vicesimo tertio, die vero mensis Augusti sep-
timo decimo.

"Per me THOMĀ, abbē de Fforda."

Seal, a stag's head caboshed.   Indorsed :

"*Recepi xxvᵗᵒ Aprilis aᵉ 1524 primam solutionem tercie partis xxxiiijͤ ͪ viiͥ iiijͩ.*"

If we would find the key to this document, which wears
the appearance, and has been referred to merely as an
acknowledgment of a simple debt, we readily discover it in
the fact that, pandering to the depraved tastes of the king,
his master, and willing at any cost to procure him the means
of continuing the indulgence of his sensual pleasures,Wolsey
was led to avail himself of his prerogative as legate *à latere*
from the pope, to extort money from the clergy,—that body
which had a natural right to look to him rather for protec-
tion and support. It was on the 15th April, 1523 (only
four months prior to the date of the abbot's letter which we
have just given) that, in order to lend the semblance of
authority to their proceeding, the king assembled parliament; convocation, according to custom, meeting at the
same time. The opportunity thus prepared was too tempt-
ing to be resisted, and Wolsey, using the influence his
character as legate gave him, succeeded, though not without
formidable opposition, in exacting a considerable subsidy
from the clergy. In this flagitious transaction is to be found

the true explanation of the foregoing letter of the Last Abbot of Ford, bearing date only the August following; and this may be regarded as the first instalment in a series of acts of spoliation, which, though the final blow was for some time deferred, was nevertheless ultimately to result in that general confiscation of the entire property of the church, by which, within a period of two years, the king became possessed of the revenues of six hundred and forty-five convents, whilst ninety colleges were demolished in several counties, two thousand three hundred and seventy-four chantries and free chapels, and one hundred and ten hospitals,—the whole revenue of these establishments, amounting to £161,000 (which was about a twentieth part of the national income), being annexed to the crown.

To return, however, more particularly to our immediate subject. The storm, long impending, had now burst upon the larger houses, and Ford Abbey was not to be exempted from the common ruin. It was on the 8th March, 1539, that Dr. Chard, with feelings doubtless ill in accord with the wording of the document, was induced to sign the surrender of his abbey. We need only look, even now, on the magnificent pile on which he had profusely lavished both his pecuniary means and the best efforts of his taste, and which must have been further endeared to him by many sacred associations, to feel assured that when he with the prior and canons assembled in the Chapter House on the aforesaid 8th March, it must have been with heavy hearts and reluctant hands that they attached their names and seals to the following document, which had been prepared beforehand for their signature, and which we here give in the form of a translated copy :

> " To all the faithful in Christ, to whom this present writing shall come : Thomas Chard, abbot of the monastery or abbacy, and of the Church of the Blessed Virgin Mary, of Ford,' in the county of Devon, of the Cistercian order, and the same place and convent, everlasting salvation in the Lord.

Per me Thomā abbem.   Know ye, that we, the aforesaid abbot and con-
Willūs Rede, prior.   vent, by our unanimous assent and consent, with
John Cosen.   our deliberate minds, right knowledge, and mere
Robte Yetmister.   motion, from certain just and reasonable causes
Johēs Newman.   especially moving our minds and consciences,

Johēs Bridgwat[r].
Thomas Stafford.
Johēs Ffawell.
W. Winsor.
Elizeus Oliscomb.
William Keynston.
William Dynyngton.
Richard Kingesbury.

have freely, and of our own accord given and granted, and by these presents do give, grant, and surrender and confirm to our most illustrious prince, Henry VIII, by the grace of God, king of England, lord of Ireland, supreme head of the Church of England in this land, all our said monastery or abbacy of Ford aforesaid. And also all and singular manors, lordships, messuages, etc. In testimony whereof, we, the aforesaid abbot and convent, have caused our common seal to be affixed to these presents. Given at our Chapter House of Ford aforesaid, on the 8th day of the month of March, and in the thirtieth year of the reign of King Henry aforesaid. Before me, William Petre, one of the clerks, etc., the day and year above written.

"By me, WILLm PETRE."

Judging by what took place in similar instances throughout the land, we may conclude that no sooner had the required signatures to the above inquitous document been obtained, than the work of destruction and pillage commenced; and though Prince states that, "by what lucky chance he knew not, Ford Abbey escaped better than its fellows, and continueth for the greatest part standing to this day," yet so manifest is the havoc that was committed even in the structure of the abbey itself, that we are rather disposed to agree with Risdon that it now merely "somewhat sheweth of what magnificence once it was." Whatever may have been the "lucky chance" which led its spoilers to spare the buildings of the abbey to the extent we now see,—whether, as before hinted, the very beauty of the fabric may not have appealed to their cupidity, and have caused it to be retained as too rich a booty to be wholly demolished,—there is now no evidence to shew: certain it is, however, that the same motives or causes, whatever they may have been, were not suffered to operate in regard to the Church of the Blessed Virgin Mary of Ford, which was at once consigned by the agents of the king to be razed to the ground,—of which in their estimation it was doubtless little else than a profitless encumbrance; and on the 28th October following the king himself, "the supreme head of the Church of England," granted the buildings, site, and precincts of the abbey, with all and singular its manors, lordships, and messuages, etc., to Richard Pollard, Esq. From this Richard Pollard,

who was subsequently knighted by Henry VIII, the Ford
Abbey estate passed to his son, Sir John Pollard, Knight,
who sold it to his first cousin, Sir Amias Poulett, of Hinton
St. George and Curry Mallet, Somerset, who, with his father
Sir Hugh Poulett, had formerly been appointed head steward
of the abbey by Dr. Chard ; which, we are told, may have
been the reason for granting the site of the abbey to Richard
Pollard, brother-in-law to Sir Hugh.[1]

Sir Amias, the father of Sir Hugh, and the grandfather of
Sir Amias the purchaser of Ford Abbey, was a benefactor
to several churches, and also to the abbey and convent of
Ford; which accounts for his arms being cut in stone on a
shield outside the cloister built by Dr. Chard.

In tracing the various changes of tenure through which
Ford Abbey with its demesne was now destined to pass, it
is a somewhat curious and interesting fact, that in the course
of about a century and a half it became the private possession of a family who were collaterally related to the Last
Abbot. From Sir Amias Poulett, Ford Abbey passed again
by purchase to William Rosewell, Esq., solicitor-general to
Queen Elizabeth; who was succeeded by his son, Sir Henry
Rosewell, who, in the year 1649, conveyed Ford Abbey to
Edmund Prideaux, Esq., the second son of Sir Edmund
Prideaux, Bart., of Netherton, Devon. Mr. Prideaux filled
the office of solicitor-general in 1648, and in the following
year was made attorney-general to Cromwell. He left one
son, Edmund Prideaux, Esq., who in 1655 married Amy
Fraunceis, coheiress of John Franceis of Comb-Florey, Somerset, Esq.; and this family of Franceis, into whose hands
Ford Abbey ultimately passed entirely, was descended, like
that of Dr. Chard, from the heirs general of William de Ivedon,—Franceis[2] from the Stanton branch, and Chard from

---

[1] History of Ford Abbey, p. 54.

[2] As has been already stated, this family of Franceis or Fraunceis was originally of Franceis Court, in the parish of Broadclist. Their arms were, *argent*,
a chevron engrailed between three mullets *gules*. Sir W. Pole tells us the arms
of "Fraunceis of Ivedon" were "the same, with a label of three *azure;* and
these arms (though they escaped the notice of Dr. Oliver) are still to be seen,
as well as the shield of the Dinhams,—*gules*, four fusils in fesse *ermine*,—in the
beautiful window of the south chantry in Awliscombe Church. Franceis Court
and the manor of Killerton Franceis are now the property of Sir T. D. Acland,
Bart., having been purchased by him of John Franceis Gwin, Esq., of Ford
Abbey, the last representative of the Franceis family   The chapel of Clyve-
land, in Awliscombe, of which no trace now remains, was licensed in favour of
this family of Franceis by Bishop Grandisson, 13th Sept., 1331, and they had
a small manor in the adjoining parish of Buckerell.

that of Tracy. In the year 1690, Margaret, the sole surviving daughter of Edmund Prideaux and his wife (Amy Frauncceis), married her cousin, Franceis Gwin, Esq., of Llansanor, Glamorganshire, who thus inherited Ford Abbey; and was ultimately succeeded in his estates by his fourth son, Franceis Gwin, who, dying without issue in 1777, devised Ford Abbey with all his other lands to his kinsman, John Frauncceis of Comb-Florey, and to his heirs male, on condition of their taking the name of Gwin; and in this family Ford Abbey remained until, at the decease of the late John Franceis Gwin, Esq., without issue, it was purchased, in September 1846, by George F. W. Miles, Esq., the present proprietor. In the year 1842, from the inconvenience of its situation for county business, an arrangement was made by which the parish of Thorncombe, containing Ford Abbey, was transferred to Dorsetshire.

The annual revenues of Ford Abbey at the time of the dissolution have been differently estimated by Dugdale and Speed, the former computing them to amount to 374*l*. : 10 : 6¼, the latter to 381*l*. : 10 : 6. In the Ecclesiastical Survey of Devon and Cornwall, returned to the crown by Veysey, bishop of Exeter, on the 3rd of November 1536, we find them recited in the following terms : " Decanus Honyton, abbatia de Forde, ubi Thomas Charde est abbas, totalis verus annuus valor tam temporalium quam spiritualium a die et anno prædictis ad 373*l*. : 11 : 0½"; and of the pensions granted in compensation to the religious of the " howse of Ford" for their lives, the whole amounted to 161*l*. : 13 : 4; of which the share of the Ex-Abbot was 80*l*. a year, together with " fourtie wayne lodes of fyre wood, to be taken yerely during his lyfe owte of suche woods being no pte of demaynes of the said late howse, as thofficers of the king's courte of the augmentacōns or there deputies for the tyme shall appoynte and assigne,"—a poor compensation truly for the loss of his dignity and position as head of such an establishment as Ford Abbey must have been at that period, and to the splendour of which he had so largely contributed.

And here it must be observed that, great as we have seen the labours and devotion of the Last Abbot, in the cause of religion, to have been, we shall form but a very imperfect notion of them if we suppose that what has here been related represents by any means their real extent, or exhibits

a full view of his numerous acts of unwearied beneficence.
We are told expressly that many of them are "undoubtedly
buried in oblivion"; and as this was stated nearly two centuries ago by so diligent an inquirer as Prince, we may well
despair of being enabled to disinter and bring them to light
at the present day.   There is, however, one instance of his
pious liberality, the record of which has been handed down
to us, and the particulars of which are deserving of a more
detailed notice.   I allude to his endowment of the leper
Hospital of St. Margaret at Honiton,—an endowment so considerable that it has raised him to an equal honour with the
original founder, with whom, indeed, it has on frequent
occasions caused him to be confounded.   No sooner was the
sumptuous restoration of his Abbey completed, than we find
him immediately directing his attention to the scene of his
birth and early life, anxious to confer on it some benefit,
and thus testify his gratitude for those advantages it had
pleased Providence to bestow upon him in this the earliest
sphere of his earthly pilgrimage.   The lazar Hospital at
Honiton, then in a lamentable state of decay, presented itself
to his notice, and seemed just suited to call forth in him
that spirit of active benevolence that was ever seeking some
fresh object on which to expend itself.   We accordingly
learn that it was in the year 1530, only two years subsequent to the completion of his Abbey, that he took upon
himself the restoration and liberal endowment of St. Margaret's Hospital in Honiton.   On the question of the original
foundation of this ancient charity both tradition and record
are alike silent.   We are indebted for the earliest notice we
have of it to the industry of the late lamented author of
the *Monasticon Diocesis Exoniensis*, who, in searching the
bishop's registers at Exeter, discovered that Bishop Bran-
tyngham, so early as 17th Sept., 1374, "granted an indulgence of twenty days to all true penitents 'qui ad susten-
tationem pauperum leprosorum hospitalis Sancte Margarite
de Honiton contulerint, donaverint aut assignaverint subsi-
dia caritatis.'"   Bishop Lacy ·(Dec. 6th, 1452) did the same
in favour of all who should contribute to the support and
relief " leprosorum virorum et mulierum in hospitali Sancte
Margarite de Honiton."   It is clear from these extracts that
the Abbot Chard was not the founder of the Hospital, though
this, as before alluded to, has been frequently asserted by

E

writers of eminence, amongst whom may be mentioned
Prince;[1] whose account, however, is in other respects the
fullest that has appeared; and as he tells us he extracted
that portion which relates to the Abbot and this endowment,
from the original grants and papers, we make no apology
for here availing ourselves of it *in extenso*. After stating
that the hospital commonly known as St. Margaret's Hospital, was situated near a quarter of a mile out of the town
of Honiton, on the east side of the road to Exeter, he proceeds :—

"It consisteth of an house with five apartments, one for the governor,
and four others for four leprous people, with an handsome chappel annexed for God's service. To the maintenance whereof the abbot limitted,
appointed, and assigned out, divers closes or parcels of land, meadow,
and pasture, lying in Honiton and Awliscombe aforesaid, for the maintenance and sustentation of the said governor and the four leprous
people of the said hospital for ever. That is to say, one close lying in
Honiton, on the east side of the way leading to Exeter, containing by
estimation two acres and three quarters; one other close thereunto
adjoyning, in Honiton aforesaid, containing by estimation three acres
and one quarter; one other close in Honiton aforesaid, lying on the
same side of the way aforesaid, containing by estimation one acre; the
chappel, messuage, orchard, and herb garden, on the same side also,
containing by estimation one yard of land; which how much that may
be is uncertain. Moreover he gave one piece of meadow ground lying
in Ottery Moor, in the said parish of Honiton, containing by estimation
half an acre; two other several pieces of ground in Honiton aforesaid,
lying on the west side of the same way, containing by estimation four
acres; one meadow adjoyning to the said messuage, containing by estimation two acres; one other close in Honiton aforesaid, lying on the
same west side of the way, containing by estimation five acres; and
one meadow, called Spittle[2] Meadow, lying in Awlescombe aforesaid,
containing by estimation one acre and a half. All which, besides the
house, garden, and orchard, amounts to about twenty acres of good
land; and, with two closes given to the said hospital by the lords of
the manor of Battishorn, in the parish of Honiton aforesaid, lying under
Gobsworthy Hill, containing about two acres, the cleer yearly value of
five and twenty pounds and six shillings. This is over and besides the
yearly head-rent reserved out of the same, viz., three.pounds of wax
and one and twenty pence; for which four shillings in money was

---

[1] Tanner also in his *Notitia*.
[2] From its connexion with the Hospital, it seems probable that this name is
merely a corruption of Spital.

agreed to be paid yearly to the heir male of this family of Chard living in Awlescombe aforesaid. To whom was likewise reserved the nomination and appointment of the said governor's place as oft as the same should become void; who, with the consent of such governor for the time being, had also the placing of all leprous persons into the said hospital upon the death or voidance of such as were formerly therein. For the nomination or admittance of any such person, twelve pence only was to be taken, and no more."[1]

It is manifest from the foregoing passage that the Abbot was anxious to connect this object of his bounty with his own birth-place and family, and that with this view he vested "the yearly head-rent" in "the heir male of this family of Chard living in Awlescomb aforesaid; to whom was likewise reserved the nomination and appointment of the said governor's place as oft as the same should become void," etc.; and that it was not, therefore, by an accidental circumstance, or any transaction connected with the dissolution of the colleges and hospitals, that the family of the Abbot "became possessed" of this Hospital, as Lysons[2] would lead us to infer, when he merely states, "after the dissolution of the colleges and hospitals, the representatives of Abbot Chard became possessed of this Hospital"; whereas the Abbot himself expressly vested the trusteeship in his own family, as we have just seen. Subsequently to the time of the Abbot this patronage remained upwards of a century in the hands of the Chard family, and was well and duly administered by them; but after this period, it appears, the affairs of the Hospital were misgoverned, and we are told that those who were appointed its trustees applied the profits of the land to their own use. A commission of pious uses was thereupon directed, composed of the following gentlemen, viz. :

Willm. Put, of Combe, Esq.	John Pole, Bart.
Hen. Fry, of Deer Park, Gent.	William Fry, of Yarty, Esq.
Peter Prideaux, Bart.	Nicholas Put, of Combe, Esq.

And from a copy of a decree of the said commissioners, bearing date 18th June, 1642, it was presented by the jury under the said commission, that the ancestors of John Chard, the then possessor of Tracy, had "had the appointment of the governor of the said Hospital as oft as the same had

[1] Prince's *Worthies*, pp. 196, 197.   [2] Vol. ii, p. 283.

become void, and the placing of all leprous persons there; and that the said Hospital had been misgoverned in the time of the said John Chard and of his father Richard Chard, and the profits of the lands of the hospital converted by them to their own use." Whereupon it was ordered that the Hospital should from that time be under the management of the rector, churchwardens, and overseers, of Honiton, who should appoint the governor and four leprous persons, or in default of such objects, other poor persons; and that neither the rector, churchwardens, overseers, nor the governor, should take any gift or reward for the admittance of any leprous or poor people to the Hospital, other than 12d. for each. At this time the jurors valued the lands of the Hospital at 25l. : 6 : 8 *per annum;* but in the year 1814 the rents had increased in value to 97l. : 2. There were originally, as Prince states, four houses besides the governor's ; but the funds of the charity having accumulated, four new houses were added in the year 1808, and since then the number of poor persons admitted has at times amounted to eleven. We ascertained that in June 1861 it was nine.

Writing of this charity in 1840, the late Dr. Oliver says : "In our account of Awliscombe we have mentioned St. Margaret's Chapel[1] in Honiton parish, and have proved its early foundation : to which, nearly two hundred years later, the Right Rev. Dr. Thos. Chard, abbot of Forde, proved himself a special benefactor......The chapel, thirty-two feet long and thirteen broad in the interior, is now in a dangerous state, and calls for immediate repair."[2] This description is now happily no longer applicable, the Chapel having of late years been put in a very decent state of repair, and the comforts of the poor attendants provided for. It was formerly the duty of the governor to read prayers to the poor persons of the Hospital in the Chapel on Wednesdays and Fridays; but

---

[1] In speaking thus of the Chapel, Dr. Oliver has somewhat failed in his usual accuracy, since neither in his own notice, nor in his extracts from the bishop's registers, is any mention of the *Chapel* to be found. In each instance it is the *hospital* only that is specified ; and Prince expressly particularises " the chapel, messuage, orchard, and herb garden, on the east side of the road leading to Exeter, containing by estimation one yard of land," as one amongst the numerous instances of the Abbot's special benefactions. We must therefore conclude that he gave the site, and rebuilt, if indeed he was not the actual founder of, the present Chapel.

[2] Ecclesiastical Antiquities, vol. ii, p. 74.

✠ SAINT : MARGARETES : HOSPITAL : AND : CHAPEL : HONITON : DEVON.

ERECTED BY ABBEE CHARD : A.D : 1530

the present governor, being incapacitated by age and in-
firmity, the duty has been undertaken by the highly esteemed
rector of Honiton, who provides that not only shall the poor
inmates have the prayers of the Church read to them on
the days appointed, but enjoy the advantage also of a lecture
afterwards,—the service, in fact, being open to any who
may please to attend it; so that this may justly be regarded
as one of those particular instances of the piety of Abbot
Chard, the memorial of which, we may still say in the words
of Prince, "hath descended to posterity with a fragrant
odour home to this day." At the eastern end of the Chapel
is a late Perpendicular window, and beneath it traces, which
evidently mark what was once the situation of the altar, on
the left hand side of which we may further discover the
remains of the credence table. The western end is divided
from the rest by a partition, and serves the purpose of a
belfry; and just beneath the apex of the western gable is a
small bell, doubtless one of the original relics of the ancient
Chapel, bearing the inscription,

"GOD PRESERVE THE HOVSE,"

intended probably as a pious valediction by the Abbot Chard,
which has to this day been so remarkably fulfilled. A view
of the Chapel and a portion of the Hospital, on the right hand
side of the road, looking towards the town, is here given.

Before quitting our notice of this Chapel, there is a circumstance connected with it for which I am disposed to
prefer the claim only of strong probability; but which,
should it ever be ascertained as a fact, would tend to invest
it with much additional interest. I refer to my belief that
this ancient Chapel was the burying-place of the Last Abbot
of Ford. Most writers are agreed as to the period of his
death, though none furnish us with any clue as to where he
was buried; and Prince, after stating that he died about the
year 1543, immediately remarks, "though where interred, I
find not." Had Thomas Chard not lived to be deprived of
his abbacy, and to see his Abbey fall into the hands of the
spoiler, there can be little doubt that his last remains would
have found their appropriate resting-place within the sacred
precincts of the Conventual Church of the Blessed Virgin
Mary of Ford; but torn, as he now was, from those associations by which his Abbey must have been endeared to him,

and stripped of his dignity as its head, what could have been more natural than that he should have desired to rest his bones in the later, though humbler and less conspicuous object of his benevolent solicitude,—the Chapel of St. Margaret's Hospital at Honiton,—to which his feelings would naturally be drawn from its close proximity to his birth-place, and from the means he took to connect its future welfare with his own family residing at Tracy in Awliscombe. It is not, however, from these considerations alone that I am induced to claim for St. Margaret's Chapel the honour of containing the last remains of this eminent and truly pious man. In his account of the chapel, published in 1840, Dr. Oliver,* after remarking on its dilapidated condition, proceeds to state, "the west door is secured within by (instead of a lock) a large sepulchral slab, to which was formerly affixed a brass plate." Now, as there is no trace of any other interment ever having taken place in this Chapel, and "a large sepulchral slab having a brass plate affixed to it," clearly indicates that it must have been placed to the memory of some one of more than ordinary note, does it not become a most natural, if not an almost legitimate conclusion, that this sepulchral slab with its brass plate (the only relic of the kind to be discovered within the edifice), recorded no other than the interment of the founder of the Chapel itself,—the venerable Ex-Abbot of Ford? As the brass plate was lost at the time Dr. Oliver saw the stone, no certain information could be gathered from it; and except some fragments, still in the same situation, formed a part of the stone itself, which, from their appearance, I can scarcely believe, all trace of the sepulchral slab itself is now gone. Unless, therefore, it should become necessary at any future period to open any portion of the floor of the Chapel, or to dig to some depth in its vicinity, there seems but small chance of ever determining whether or not the Chapel of St. Margaret's Hospital, Honiton, contains, as I am inclined to think, the tomb of its founder, the Last Abbot of Ford.

With the exception of his Abbey and the Hospital of St. Margaret at Honiton, the remaining monuments of Dr. Chard's taste and pious generosity, which time has suffered to descend to us, are now comparatively few even in his own county. Although I confess I have been unable to dis-

* Ecclesiastical Antiquities in Devon, vol. ii, p. 74.

cover any record that will lend the sanction of authority to
the opinion, I am on several accounts strongly disposed to
believe that we are, in a measure at all events, indebted to
his taste for the very beautiful aisle or chapel communicat-
ing with the north aisle of the nave of Ottery Church, which
has so often been made the subject of graphic description.
In a note to a paper by John Duke Coleridge, Esq., M.A.,
read before the Exeter Diocesan Architectural Society, 11th
Sept., 1851, we are told that "there are strong grounds for
fixing the date of the erection of this aisle or chapel between
the years 1503 and 1530,—that is, between 19 Henry VII
and 21 Henry VIII. Independently of its architectural
character, we have in the porch the arms of Oldham, who
presided over the see from 1507 to 1523; and on one of
the corbels within the aisle, those of Veysey, who succeeded
him." From the occurrence thus, then, of the arms of bishops
Oldham and Veysey, there can be little doubt that the building of this aisle was in progress in their day, during the
time we know Dr. Chard to have been their Suffragan, and
their most intimate friend and ally,—more particularly of
Oldham. We further know that he was the Warden of the
College at Ottery from 9th Oct. 1513, to 16th Oct. 1518,
and that during this period the work must have been con-
stantly under his immediate observation. What, therefore,
can be more probable than that he should have taken some
part in influencing and promoting a work so congenial to
his taste, and which has been described as being "perhaps
the grandest specimen of the florid and most recent style of
English architecture within the diocese of Exeter"? That
there existed some cause which induced him to feel a special
interest in this Church, there can be no question, inasmuch
as it is mentioned as one of the particular objects to which
he became a benefactor under his will.

It is, however, in the church of his native parish that we
must seek for the last remaining instance that can be relied
on of the taste and munificence of Dr. Chard. I have the
authority of Dr. Oliver for stating that the beautiful South
Porch of the parish Church of Awliscombe, and also the
glorious south window of the South Chantry there, are both
the work of Thomas Chard, the Last Abbot of Ford; though
at what precise period of his life they were executed I find
no account. When Dr. Oliver first visited the church he

described the groining and ornaments of the porch as having been encrusted and choked with whitewash; which, however, was removed some years since by the good taste of the present vicar, so that it now appears in all its original beauty. A drawing of this beautiful window, together with the porch, as seen from the exterior, is here given. On entering the Church, and passing into the Chantry Chapel, the south window, "with its gorgeous tabernacle-work," at once commands our admiration. In the east window of this Chantry is a figure of St. Roch, as a mendicant, on crutches; and further, to the north-east, may be observed the Hagioscope, now walled up.

From the time of the surrender of his Abbey, the days of the last Abbot appear to have passed unmarked by any incident of note. We have seen that the only preferment he received after that date was to the office of Minister of Ottery Church. Being then advanced in age, he resigned this appointment in the year 1543; and the early part of the following year, 1544, is the date assigned by general consent as that at which the death of this eminent man took place. And that it must have occurred just at this period is placed beyond doubt by the fact that, in his Vicarage of Thorncombe (then void by his death) he was succeeded by William Freke on the 20th May, 1544; whilst his will, which bears date 1st October, 1541, was proved in the Prerogative Court of Canterbury on the 4th Nov., 1544. Although, as formerly hinted, it appears the Will itself is now no longer to be found, we learn from various sources that he became a benefactor by it to the Church of "St. Mary Otery in Devon," and also the Churches of St. Mary Magdalen in Taunton, and St. John the Baptist at Wellington in Somersetshire; whilst Wood mentions likewise the Church of "Holberton" in the latter county,—in mistake, as I imagine, for Holbeton in Devon, the vicarage of which he held for about two years, as we have already seen.

After the death of the Abbot, the other incidental notices of this family of Chard are not numerous, yet they are quite sufficient to furnish evidence of the fact before adverted to, that the family continued at Tracy, in Awliscombe, for a period of about four hundred years, viz., from the beginning of the fifteenth down to the end of the eighteenth century. Not long after the death of the Abbot we find Tracy in the

THE SOUTH TRANSEPT AND PORCH
OF SAINT MICHAEL, AWLISCOMBE, DEVON.
ERECTED BY ABBOT GUARD, CIRCA 1435.

possession of his nephew, or great-nephew, Richard Chard ; of whom, together with other members of the family, sundry notices are to be found in the Awliscombe Register and elsewhere. We find that " William Chard, the sonne of Richard Chard, was baptised the ffirst day of ffebruarie, 1589." " Marie Chard, the daughter of Richard Chard, was baptised the 16th daie of April, 1592." Humphry Chard was buried the 28th daic of April, 1629. It was in 1642, as we have seen, that a commission of charitable uses was directed against John Chard, son of the aforesaid Richard Chard, for his maladministration of the affairs of St. Margaret's Hospital in Honiton. Mrs. Johan Chard was buried the 13th day of July, 1645. A Thomas Chard was buried the 16th June, 1676, in the north or Tracy aisle of Awliscombe Church, where, on a tombstone, forming part of the pavement of the aisle, his name and the date of his interment are still visible. The stone appears to have borne the Chard arms and a lengthened inscription, which, however, the passage of feet over it for nearly two hundred years, has all but obliterated. In 1690, Daniel Pring of Ivedon married Mary Chard of Tracy, and the descendants of this marriage are now the only remaining representatives of this family of Chard; whilst it may be remarked as an interesting fact, that the family of De Ivedon, from whom this Mary Chard was in a direct line descended, may be regarded as having been thus, in her person, reinstated in the possession of their original estate, which, as we have already seen, they held at the Conquest.

In the year 1701, when the first edition of Prince's *Worthies* appeared, he states, speaking of Tracy, that " in that name (Chard) it continueth this day." Hannah Chard was buried the 6th March, 1753; and the writer of these pages has in his possession a deed bearing date 1748, in which the name of " John Chard of Tracyshays, within the parish of Awliscombe, in the county of Devon, gentleman," occurs as one of the principal parties concerned. This John Chard was born in 1712, and died in April 1753. The names of his widow Catherine Chard, and his brother-in-law, John Lewis of Plymouth, occur in a subsequent deed. In Polwhele's *History of Devon*, written about the year 1790, it is stated that " the late Mr. John Charde, the last male branch of the family, gave his estate (of Tracy) to his sister's son, John Charde Lewis, a minor, for whom his father, John

F

Lewis, built a house at Tracy. John Charde Lewis died a bachelor; and the estate, by purchase, became the property of Jenkins."[1] All of which affords sufficient evidence, it is presumed, that this family of Chard held the estate of Tracy, the Abbot's birth-place, for a period of just four hundred years.[2]

In concluding this imperfect sketch of the subject of this Memoir, I am sensible that in having ventured to carry the attention of my readers into a path of research so foreign to my ordinary pursuits, I stand in more than common need of their kind indulgence. The apprehension, however, that all authentic information respecting the Last Abbot of Ford was rapidly passing away, and even his very name becoming involved in doubt, induced me to endeavour to collect and arrange the many scattered notices which occur of him, into a fuller and more exact account than any previously existing. Although, as stated in the outset, his character presents few or no points of dazzling brilliancy, yet it commends itself no less to our regard by its plain, intrinsic worth. From the numerous notices of him which we have found to be still in existence, we are unable to gather that he ever made an enemy,—or, at least, we can discover none who have been willing to chronicle any ill of him; whilst on the other hand we have seen that, at the most distracting epoch in the history of the Church, and at a time when every effort was made to overwhelm its ministers with the weight of accumulated odium, he was still to be found at the post of duty in the unwearied exercise of practical benevolence, and devoting the best energies of a long and active life to the service of religion; so that, on a survey of his character, Prince records him as being "an ornament to our country"; whilst in reference to the account here offered of him, the writer feels constrained to add that he was undoubtedly "worthy of a more worthy pen to have preserved his memory and commended his merits to the imitation of posterity."

[1] Note at p. 328.
[2] A marked contrast to the frequent changes of tenure which the Ford Abbey property has undergone; in respect of which it has proved no exception to the common observation, that, "either through sale, through default of issue, or, in many instances, through greater and more grievous disaster," the receivers of the plunder of the Church have rarely retained it in possession for any lengthened period.